The Lighthouse Keeper's Mystery

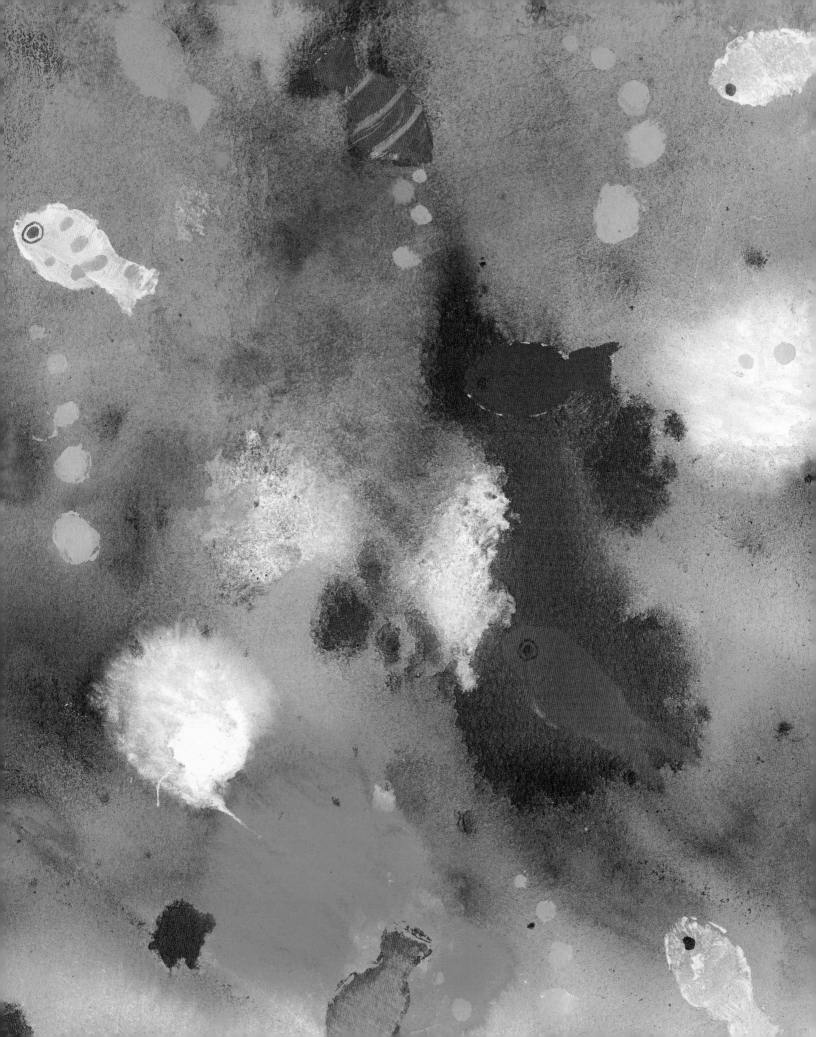

To Tomas and all the other
Lighthouse Keeper book
readers, wherever they are.

This edition first published in 2020 by Scholastic Children's Books
Euston House, 24 Eversholt Street, London NW1 1DB
a division of Scholastic Ltd
www.scholastic.co.uk

London ~ New York ~ Toronto ~ Sydney ~ Auckland ~ Mexico City ~ New Delhi ~ Hong Kong

PB ISBN 978 1407 1938 54
C&F ISBN 978 0702 3022 68

The Lighthouse
Keeper's Mystery

RONDA AND DAVID ARMITAGE

SCHOLASTIC

Mr and Mrs Grinling lived with their cat, Hamish, in a little white cottage perched high on the cliffs. Mr Grinling was a retired lighthouse keeper, and he still kept the lighthouse spick and span for the visitors who came to look around.

As it was holiday time, the Grinlings' great-nephew,
George, had come to stay.

Mrs Grinling was bustling around the kitchen.
"Eat faster, you two. It's market day for Sally,
so I'm in charge of Sally's Café," she said.

"George can help me at the lighthouse,"
said Mr Grinling.

"The first job is a clean up," said Mr Grinling. "Could you please polish the light, George? Hamish can check for mice, and I'll pick up that rubbish on the rocks."

"Where it all comes from is a mystery to me," muttered Mr Grinling. He filled the basket and sent it off down the wire.

Seagulls Yvette, Rita and Gus spotted the basket.

"Great work, George," said Mr Grinling. "Now it's time to tackle the beach."

"Picking up rubbish on my first day, that's not fair," complained George. "Everybody should pick up their *own* rubbish, and then it wouldn't end up in the water."

"You're right," said Mr Grinling, "but there's so much here, I think some of this rubbish has been dumped out at sea."

"But what about the sea creatures, Uncle G.?"

Deep down below, all was not well.
Lobster's claw was caught in a
baked-bean can.

Shark had chewed an old lilo and now
it was stuck in her sharp teeth.

Baby seal couldn't catch any breakfast. He was tangled in old plastic fishing nets.

Octopus had to bundle plastic straws and yoghurt pots out of her house.

Very early on Wednesday morning, Mr Grinling noticed something strange out at sea.

Very early on Thursday morning, Mr Grinling peered again.

On Friday morning, Mr Grinling
woke George.

"See that boat, George? This is the third
morning it's been there by Tiny Island.
I think it's dumping rubbish. We must
catch them."

"It's probably trash pirates," said George.
"I know a thing or two about pirates,
Uncle G. I'd better take my sword."

As the sun was rising, Mr Grinling, George and
Hamish put out to sea. The *Kittiwake* putted gently
through the white-tipped waves.

"No dolphins?" asked George.

Mr Grinling shook his head. "No dolphins, George, not for a long time. Once the sea is cleared of rubbish, they might return."

"I can hear something," said George.

Putt, putt, putt, putt, putt, putt…

Mr Grinling nudged the *Kittiwake* near the rocks.

"Ahoy there!" shouted George, waving his sword.

"Sit down, George! You'll fall in!" said Mr Grinling sternly.

Too late! The *Kittiwake* hit a rock, but it was Mr Grinling who fell – SPLASH – head over heels into the sea.

George didn't notice. It was Hamish who threw out a rope. George was too busy yelling…

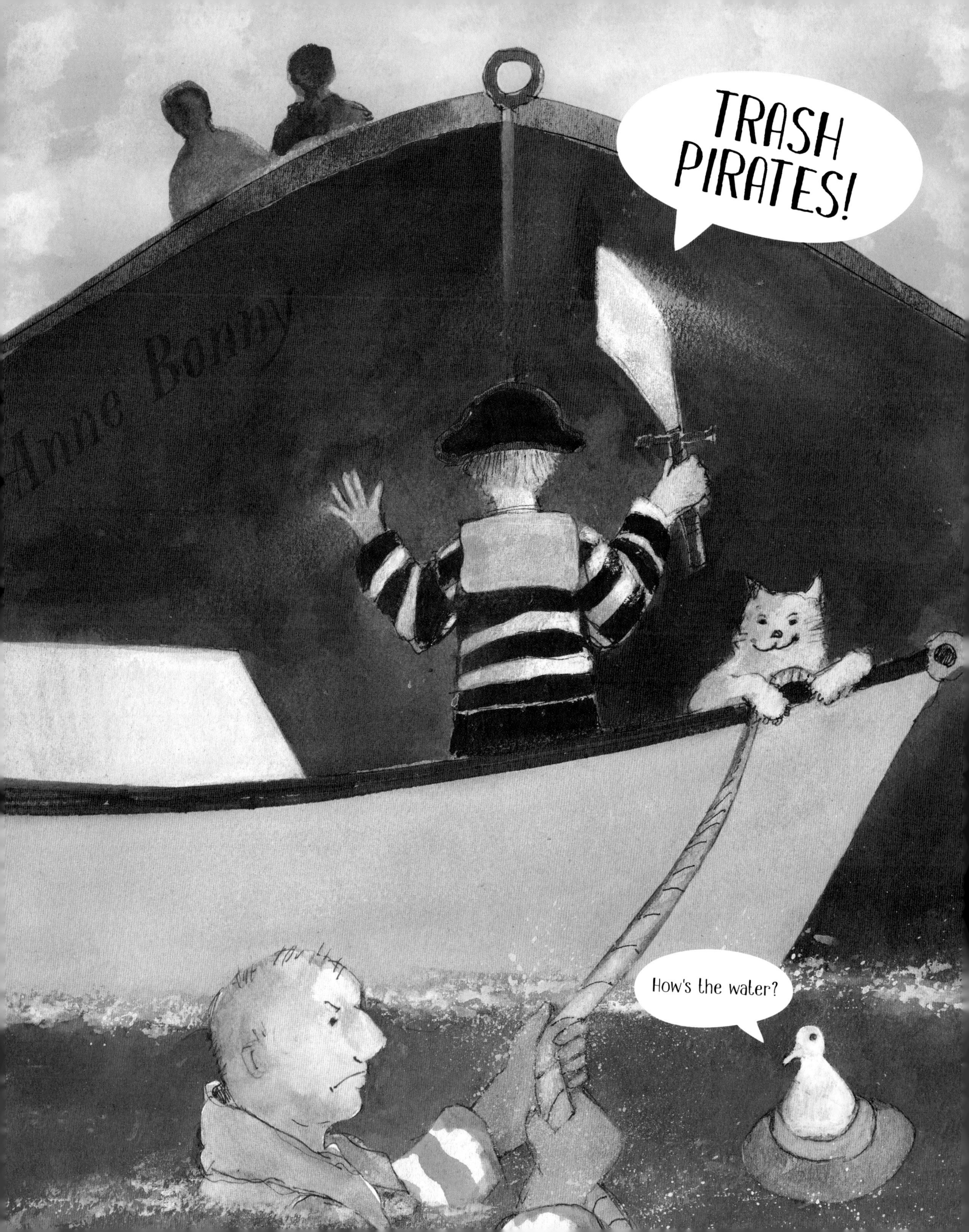
Anne Bonny
TRASH PIRATES!
How's the water?

"Not trash pirates, we're fisherfolk," called a voice, and Captain Cod invited Mr Grinling and George onboard. "I don't throw plastic rubbish in the sea, I fish it out. More plastic than fish!"

George pulled a plastic bag from the rubbish. "Uncle G., look at this turtle! It can't get out!"

George lifted the bag very carefully. The turtle didn't move.

"The poor fellow. We'll take him back to the beach to show everyone," said Mr Grinling.

At the beach, Mr Grinling called out, "Please gather round, everyone! Sea creatures get hurt when our plastic rubbish goes into the sea. Like this fellow here!"

Once everyone had seen the turtle, George laid him gently in the water.

Bye, little turtle!

Mr Grinling set up a very large recycling bin.
He and Jason the postman painted it.

Sally and Mrs Grinling put
up posters at the café.

The seagulls snatched some
lunch from a basket.

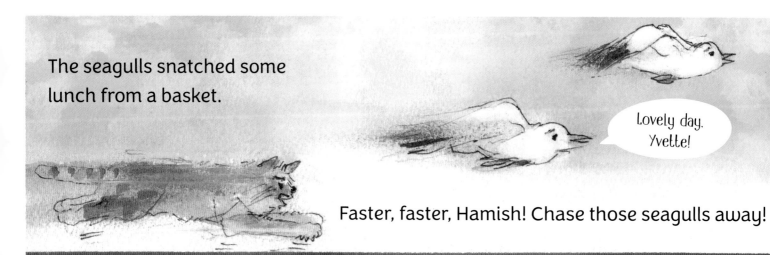

Faster, faster, Hamish! Chase those seagulls away!

At the end of the week, everyone had collected all the rubbish from the beach. Mr Grinling was appointed the new Beach Warden, making sure the beach stayed rubbish free.

"Three cheers!" he cried. "And now it's time for the Clean Beach Barbecue!"

While the grown-ups cooked, the children played with the clean, wet sand.

It was a glorious barbecue.

Later, as the sun set, the children splashed
in the waves, but not until every piece of
rubbish had been put into the sea.

NO, NO, NO!

Into the bins?

YES!

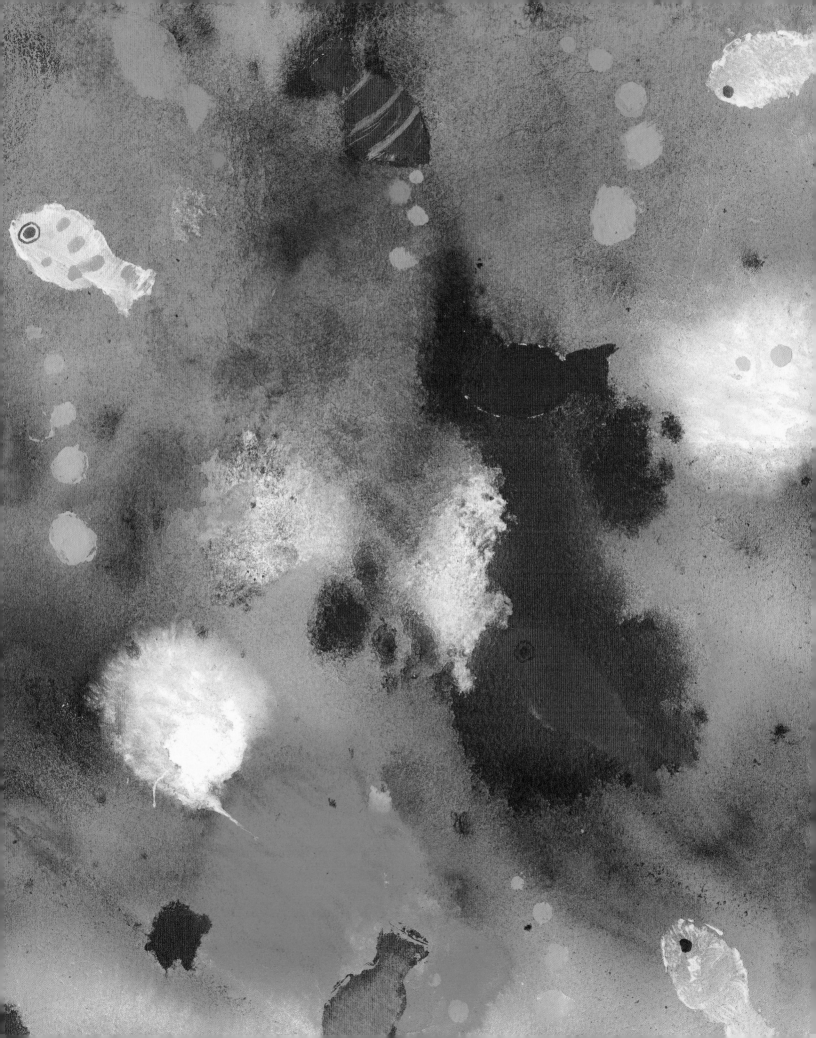